Zimbabwe (Rhodesian Ridgeback)

Like Australia, Zimbabwe (Zim to the locals) enjoys hot weather at Christmastime. So Zimbabweans share the holidays with brightly colored flame lilies and feathered friends like go-away birds and paradise flycatchers. You can't enjoy a Zim Christmas without singing and dancing.

Merry Kisimusi

Netherlands (Keeshond)

Snickerdoodle means "little cake," from the Dutch *keokje*. The simple cinnamon-spiced cookie became popular in America about a century ago. Equally whimsical names include jumbles, plunkets, and even cry babies. Children in Holland (also called the Netherlands) may leave out a few Snickerdoodles for St. Nick (*Sinterklaas* in Dutch).

Gelukkig Kerstfeest

Germany (Affenpinscher)

Where did the Christmas pickle tradition come from? Some place its origin in Germany, but Germans aren't so quick to claim it. Wherever it came from, it lives on ... and the lucky kid to find it hidden deep in the Christmas tree gets to claim an extra gift!

Fröhliche Weihnachten

Turkey (Kangal)

Today, most Turkish people don't celebrate Christmas. But in the town of Demre, St. Nicholas's birth is recognized with a three-day celebration each year. He is remembered for his kindness to children everywhere. For those in Turkey who do celebrate Christmas, Santa Claus is *Noel Baba*, or Father Christmas.

Mutlu Noeller

Italy (Neapolitan Mastiff)

Italy is also noteworthy for its "living crèches" (*presepi viventi*), where people dress up to act out the parts of the Nativity. In Chia, near Soriano in northern Italy, the town holds a large living Nativity on December 26 with more than 500 participants. *Mamma Mia*, that's a lot of shepherds!

Buon Natale

First Dog's White House Christmas

J. Patrick Lewis and Beth Zappitello
Illustrated by Tim Bowers

Once upon a time there was a dog

that had found the perfect place to live.

One day, as he awoke from his nap, Dog happened to see ...

Hey, thought Dog. I have friends all over the world—I'll invite them, too!

Wow! exclaimed Dog. Imagine all the planning that goes into this holiday celebration ...

... and I'll be the official Tour Guide! Dog imagined himself leading the guests around and saying, Ah, the Blue Room, my fellow bowwows. And the official White House Christmas tree is more than 18 feet tall. She's a beaut, isn't she? We have almost 50 trees in and around the White House.

Behold, the East Room. Dog was practicing his speech in his head as he walked from room to room. Wag your tails for this lavish Nativity scene and the four fireplaces hung with garlands. Mother Nature's all over the place with hydrangea, magnolia branches, honeysuckle vine, cranberries, and pine cones!

Ready to drool, you lapdogs? Look!

The Master Chef's masterpiece for the State Dining Room is a 56-by-29-inch, 390-pound white chocolate gingerbread White House, including the vegetable garden on the South Lawn. The chandelier really works and the furniture is made of dark chocolate.

Hey, who's that handsome fellow? Yep, that's me sitting right in front. I'm made of marzipan, just like the vegetables in the garden!

So much for their planning! thought Dog. Now it's time for me to put my best paw forward and come up with my own to-do list! Let's see:

1. Plan a Doggie Dash on the South Lawn
2. Gift wrap "Give-a-Dog-a-Bone" party favors
3. Draw a map of approved Rose Garden potty spots
4. Hang cat ornaments on the Christmas tree
5. Help Chef frost Dawg sugar cookies

At last, the evening of the Christmas Gala finally arrived!
Dog took his place in the reception line in the Grand Foyer.

"The White House welcomes you!" said Dog. "As you come through the
line, please tell us all about Christmas traditions in your country."

The first visitor waddled up—the English Bulldog.

"Here, Dog," he said, "chow down on our famous English gingerbread. By the way, did you know that Christmas cards got started in London in 1843, thanks to one Sir Henry Cole? The very first card read: 'A Merry Christmas and a Happy New Year to You.'"

He handed Dog some mistletoe to hang. "And that's not all. England was the first country to use this little green leaf at Christmas. The trouble is, no one will stand under the kissletoe with me."

Imagine that, thought Dog.

England

But the next dog in line was wearing a disguise over his big furry face.

"Guess who!" said the visitor. "A Saint Bernard?" said Dog.

The visitor shook his head. "I'm a Newfoundland from Canada!
This is what we do at Christmas. It's called mummering. We
wear disguises, knock on doors, and sing songs. That's me,
I'm a mummer.

"And I brought you a fruitcake. Christmas
wouldn't be Christmas in Canada without it.
Do you like fruitcake?"

Dog took a bite and made a face.
"Uh, not so much," he groaned.

Newfoundland (Canada)

Who else would come from France but the French Poodle?

"*Bonjour!*" she oozed. "In France, the kiddies set their shoes by the fireplace in hopes that *Père Noël* will leave presents in them. Now may I present you with the traditional *Bûche de Noël*—a Christmas log? It's a cake served on Christmas Eve."

"*Oui, oui,* a French pastry," Dog said, licking his chops. "What do you wish *Père Noël* would bring you?"

"Ooh, *chéri,* a blow dryer!"

France

The Australian guest looked a little worn out from his long trip.

"If it isn't the Dingo from Down Under," Dog howled. "You've traveled far, Ding-Dong. If you weren't celebrating the holiday with me, what would you be doing?"

"We live below the equator," Dingo yipped. "We're hot when you're cold. So we celebrate Christmas in summer, and that means a picnic followed by a game of cricket on the beach."

Hmmm, thought Dog, sounds perfect! (NOTE TO SELF: Work on getting an invite to next December's Dingo Doggie Dash Down Under.)

Australia

A tiny friend arrived from sunny Mexico.
"*Hola, Señorita!*" said Dog.

The Chihuahua handed him two presents:
a poinsettia and a *piñata*.

"They say that the poinsettia plant formed
miraculously one Christmas Eve when a little girl
gave a gift of weeds to the baby Jesus," said the Chihuahua. "And what's
a Mexican Christmas without a *piñata*? Children use a stick to break it
open, sending candy and toys flying everywhere. Here's a *piñata* in the
shape of a cat!"

Dog bubbled with joy, singing, "It's beginning to look a lot like Kittenmas ..."

Mexico

The elegant Rhodesian Ridgeback stepped forward, his muscles rippling.

"Christmas is a summer holiday for us, too!" he said. "It's almost always sunny in my country, Zimbabwe—children are out caroling on Christmas Day. Dinner is an open-air lunch of bread, jam, tea, and, uh, goat meat. Then families go out to the country to play games and enjoy the sunshine."

Then Ridge added, "My favorite Christmas carol is 'Bark, the Herald Beagles Sing!' What's yours?"

Dog sang out, "'The Twelve Dogs of Christmas.'"

Zimbabwe

The dainty miss from Germany scampered in—the Affenpinscher.

"As you know," said the Affen, "the first Christmas tree originated in Germany! Children are not allowed to see the tree until Christmas Eve when it's decorated with apples, nuts, cookies, angels, cars, trains, tinsel, oh, and a couple of dog bones.

"Stick out your paw," she said. Then she handed Dog a big surprise!

"A glass pickle?" Dog asked.

"That's the last ornament hung on the tree in Germany. The first child to find it gets an extra present!"

Dog snapped, "Lucky kid!"

Germany

The visitor from Italy, the Neapolitan Mastiff, had a face that looked like a map of the Alps—without the snow.

Dog asked, "Who first thought of the crèche—the Nativity scene?"

"Well," said the Mastiff, "in 1223 in the village of Greccio, Italy, Francis of Assisi hoped people would celebrate Christmas together. Since the Infant had none of the comforts babies normally receive, he made a manger out of hay, brought an ox and a donkey, and created the first crèche. Everyone who saw it that night was touched by the sight."

Dog said proudly, "Our own Italian crèche in the East Room was donated more than 30 years ago. That's 210 in dog years!"

Italy

The national dog of Holland, the Keeshond, eagerly told her story about a famous cookie.

"Compliments to your chef, Dog! He has set out Snickerdoodles on all the White House tables. Your New England cookbooks used to call them Graham Jakes, Jolly Boys, Bramble, Tangle Breeches, and Kinkawoodles. But a Snickerdoodle by any other name is still a Dutch Snickerdoodle, after the place where it was first created."

"Good to know, Madame Keeshond," said Dog. "All I ever call a Snickerdoodle is deeee-licious."

Holland (Netherlands)

Up strutted the Kangal Dog from Turkey. Why was he barking? "No need to yap in the White House, fella," said the host.

"But I'm so proud," the Kangal Dog explained. "St. Nicholas was born in my country hundreds of years ago. Known as Nicholas the Wonderworker, he was the secret gift giver who became the model for Santa Claus.

"Once there was a nobleman who had left his daughters penniless. One night they hung their clean stockings above the fireplace to dry, and went to bed. When St. Nicholas came upon the poor household, he flung three bags of gold down the chimney. They landed in the stockings. The daughters awoke the next morning to discover these riches!"

"Wow!" said Dog. "Go ahead. Bark as much as you want!"

Turkey

"Now I'd like to share with my four-legged friends one of my favorite traditions from right here in the United States ... a creamy bowl of eggnog.

It's our special holiday drink made of eggs, cream, cinnamon, and nutmeg.
A toast to all! Is everyone ready?" shouted Dog. "Then let the party begin!"

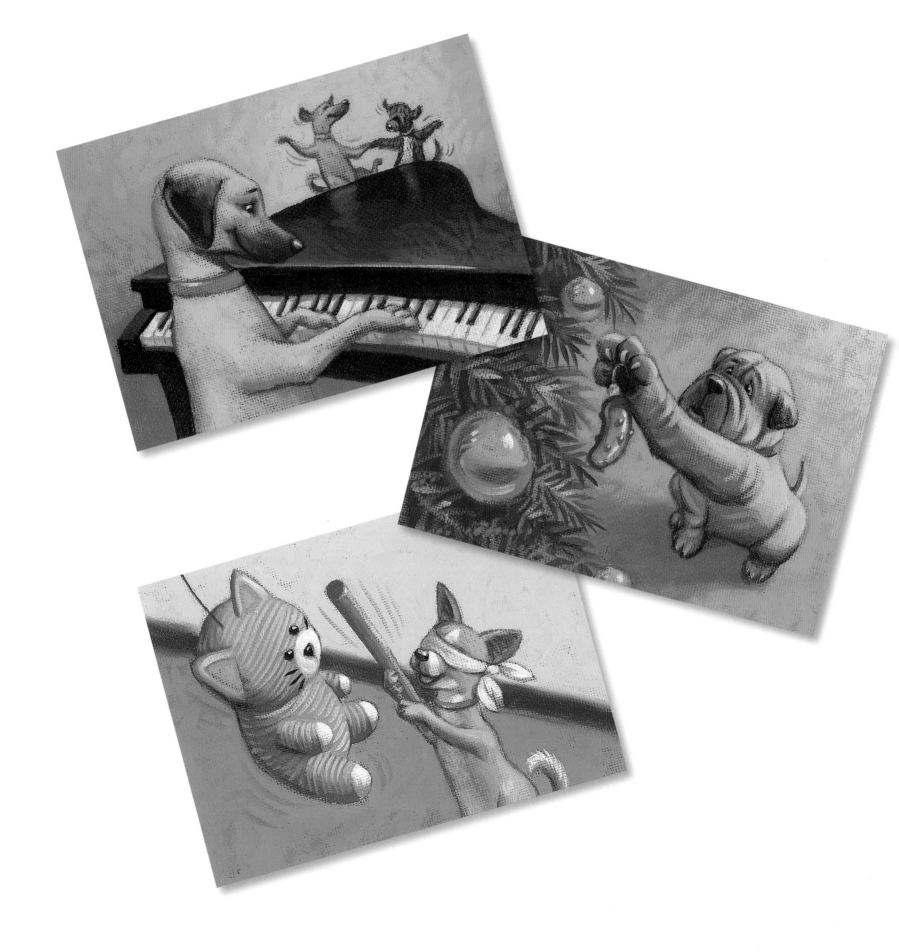

Hours later, after all the guests had gone to bed, Dog was exhausted.
He lay down on his favorite spot and was soon fast asleep.

When Dog awoke, he saw that somebody had left him a note.

Bo-ho-ho . . .

and a Merry Christmas to all!

If we thought holiday traditions were the same the world over, *First Dog's White House Christmas* brought all sorts of surprises! From Santa's various names to differences in gift giving, decoration, and, of course, that delicious holiday smorgasbord.

But the meaning of Christmas is the same for people and pooches everywhere: giving.

Every dog gives a gift that is both free and priceless at the same time—unconditional love.

At Christmastime, no matter how much or how little you have to give, you, too, can give love. And if for any reason you should forget how, lessons are always available at your nearest dog shelter.

★ ★ ★

Once again, for the many devoted members
of the animal rescue community—
J.P.L.

To the ones I love spending Christmas with,
especially Ajax and Hopper!
B.Z.

To my good friend Pat—with thanks,
and to fellow dog lovers everywhere.
T.B.

Sleeping Bear Press™ · Sleeping Bear Press is an imprint of Gale, a part of Cengage Learning · 315 East Eisenhower, Suite 200, Ann Arbor, MI 48108 · www.sleepingbearpress.com · Text Copyright © 2010 J. Patrick Lewis and Beth Zappitello · Illustration Copyright © 2010 Tim Bowers. · All rights reserved. No part of this book may be reproduced in any manner without the express written consent of the publisher, except in the case of brief excerpts in critical reviews and articles. · Printed and bound in China. · 10 9 8 7 6 5 4 3 2 1 · Library of Congress Cataloging-in-Publication Data · Lewis, J. Patrick. · First Dog's White House Christmas / written by J. Patrick Lewis and Beth Zappitello · illustrated by Tim Bowers. · p. cm. · Summary: The dog that lives at the White House invites international guests to a Christmas party, where they share holiday customs from their respective countries. · ISBN 978-1-58536-503-6 · [1. Dogs—Fiction. 2. Christmas—Fiction. 3. Parties—Fiction. 4. White House (Washington, D.C.)—Fiction.] I. Zappitello, Beth. II. Bowers, Tim, ill. III. Title. · PZ7.L5866Fi 2010 · [E]—dc22 · 2010011854

NOV 17 2010

England (English Bulldog)

Can mistletoe work miracles? For the ancient Romans, who occupied England for nearly 400 years, enemies who met under a sprig of it sometimes declared a truce and went home. In Anglo-Saxon, *mistel* meant 'dung,' and *tan* was a word for 'twig.' So, mistletoe means 'dung-on-a-twig.' How romantic!

Merry Christmas

Australia (Dingo)

Australia's immigrants came from England and Ireland and brought their customs with them. Since the seasons on the smallest continent are opposite ours, families enjoy surfing, sailing, bike-riding, or watching cricket, but most of them fire up summer's backyard grill for a shrimp-on-the-barbie Christmas dinner, topped off with a flaming plum pudding dessert.

Happy (or Merry) Christmas

Newfoundland (Newfoundland)

If you are visiting Newfoundland over Christmas, you had better remember your disguise as it's customary to go "mummering" at friends and neighbors (not to be confused with Halloween trick-or-treating). Of course, you'll be really welcome if you bring a Canadian favorite ... fruitcake!

Merry Christmas

Mexico (Chihuahua)

On December 16, the Mexican Christmas called *las posadas* begins with a piñata party—the children's favorite. When this nine-day portrayal of the journey to Bethlehem ends, Mexico rejoices in *Buena Noche* (Christmas Eve). After Midnight Mass, fireworks light the night sky, and children receive presents from Santa Claus.

Feliz Navidad

France (Poodle)

A 1962 French law requires *Père Noël* to send a postcard to any child who writes a letter to him. When an elementary school class sends a letter, each student can expect to get a response. (The French Santa must spend most of the year at his writing desk!)

Joyeux Noël

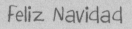